Eli
A Black Bear

by
Bonnie Highsmith Taylor

Perfection Learning®

Cover Photo: Gary and Sharon Alt
Photographs courtesy of Gary and Sharon Alt: pp. 11, 16–17,
18, 19, 21, 26, 28, 33, 37, 39, 43, 47, 49, 53.
Some images copyright www.arttoday.com
Book Design: Randy Messer

Dedication

To my aunt, Wanda Fitzgerald

About the Author

Bonnie Highsmith Taylor is a native Oregonian. She loves
camping in the Oregon mountains and watching birds and
other wildlife. Writing is Ms. Taylor's first love. But she
also enjoys going to plays and concerts, collecting antique
dolls, and listening to good music.

Paperback 0-7891-2937-x
Cover Craft® 0-7807-8967-9

2 3 4 5 6 PP 06 05 04 03 02

4

Contents

Chapter 1

It was getting very cold. The leaves had fallen from the trees. The summer birds had flown south. Small animals had burrowed deep into the ground.

It had snowed hard for over a week. It was time for bears to den for winter.

A young female black bear walked through the woods. She was looking for a den. A safe, warm place to spend the winter.

She came to a hollow log. She sniffed it all over. She put her head inside. It was much too small.

On she went. As she searched, she grew sleepier and sleepier.

At last, the she-bear found a deep hole where a tree had blown over. It was sheltered by the tree's roots.

For days, she carried dead leaves and limbs into the hole. She made a snug winter bed.

For days, she ate and ate. The food would turn to fat. The fat would last all winter. It would keep her from needing food until spring.

Before going to sleep for the winter, a bear must put on fat. Lots of fat. Sometimes the fat on a bear's back will be five inches thick.

A few days before denning, the she-bear

stopped eating food.

She then ate pine needles, bark, and even bits of her own hair. These passed through her stomach. It made an anal plug. No body waste could be passed until spring. That was when she'd leave the den.

The bear crawled down into the hole. She turned herself around and around. The den was warm and cozy. The she-bear made soft grunting sounds. She grew sleepier and sleepier.

Her heartbeat dropped from 55 beats a minute to about 35 beats a minute. Her temperature dropped from 100 degrees to about 95 degrees.

This would be the she-bear's third winter alone. She had not seen her mother or twin brother for over two years.

Her first winter, she had denned with her mother and twin brother. The year before, she and her brother had been born in a hollow tree stump.

Now she was three and one-half years old. In midsummer she had mated. Around the first of February, she would give birth. For the first time.

Outside, the wind blew. Snow fell deep. The temperature dropped below zero.

Now and then, a coyote or a pack of wolves howled in the distance. The young bear stirred a little. But she slept on.

Once, a herd of elk passed by the den. Searching for food.

But inside the snug den, the she-bear slept soundly.

Chapter 2

The first week in February, Eli was born. He weighed eight ounces. He was the size of a rat.

Eli's mother weighed nearly 200 pounds. When Eli was fully grown, he would weigh between 300 and 400 pounds. Males weigh much more than females.

A bear gains more weight from birth to adulthood than any animal. Except animals that are kept in pouches, like possums.

Eli was born blind. His eyes would not open until he was about six weeks old. He looked hairless. And he had no teeth. But he had tiny, sharp claws.

The first thing Eli did was find a nipple and nurse. A female bear has six nipples. Four on her chest between her front legs. And two between her hind legs.

Eli had no brothers or sisters. Bears usually have only one cub the first time they give birth. After that, they usually

have twins or triplets. There have been
a few cases of litters of five or six.
Bears have cubs every two or three
years.

Eli was born with almost no tail. There
is a legend about how the bear lost his
tail.

Long ago, a bear was fishing on the
ice. He was fishing with his long tail.
His tail dangled in the cold water. It
hung through a hole in the ice.

When a big fish grabbed hold of it,
the frozen tail fell off. From then on,
bears had no tails.

Of course, this is just a story. But some ancestors of the bear did have long tails. Bearlike animals lived about 28 million years ago in Asia and Europe. They were very large animals with long furry tails.

During the Ice Age, about 25,000 years ago, there were cave bears. They were the size of present-day grizzly bears.

These bears lived on earth before humans came. When they appeared, these bears were all killed. They have been extinct for thousands of years.

In the past, there were hundreds of different kinds of bears. Now there are only eight kinds.

Alaskan brown bears and polar bears are the largest. They are eight to eleven feet long. The grizzly bear is also about eight feet long.

Interesting Bear Facts

Type	Length	Weight	Color	Home
Alaskan Brown Bears	up to 10 feet	up to 1,700 pounds	brown	Alaska and the surrounding islands
American Black Bears	5 feet	200 to 300 pounds	black, rusty brown, white, and a bluish color	North America
Asiatic Bears	5 feet	250 pounds	black with a moon-shaped mark on their chests	Asia
European Brown Bears/ Grizzly Bears	up to 9 feet	800 pounds	brown to blackish brown fur with white tips	Europe, Asia, and western North America
Polar Bears	9 feet to 11 feet	600 to 1,500 pounds	white with a hint of yellow	regions bordering on the Arctic Ocean
Sloth Bears	5 feet	250 pounds	shaggy black fur and a white or yellow chest mark shaped like a U, V, or Y	India and Sri Lanka
Spectacled Bears	5 feet	200 to 300 pounds	shaggy black or brown fur	mountains of northwestern South America
Sun Bears	3 feet	60 to 100 pounds	black coat, a gray or orange nose, and a yellow chest mark like a sun	the forests of Borneo, Indochina, the Malay Peninsula, Sumatra, and Thailand

15

The American black bear, the Asiatic black bear, the sloth bear, and the spectacled bear are about five feet long. The smallest bear is the sun bear. It is three feet long.

Eli spent most of his time sleeping and nursing. His mother woke often to wash her cub. She also licked the urine and feces from his body. This kept the den clean.

Even in her sleep, the mother bear
made soft sniffling sounds. This
comforted her cub. Little Eli whimpered.
He snuggled deep in her soft, warm fur.

As Eli nursed, he pawed against his
mother's breast. This made the milk
flow faster. If his sharp little claws
scratched too hard, the she-bear gave a
low growl.

Weeks passed. Eli grew very fast. He began to cut teeth. He grew hair. It was soft and fine.

At last, after nearly six weeks, his eyes opened. It was hard to see in the dark den. But after a while, he was able to find his way about.

He climbed on his mother. He nipped her ears. He growled playfully. His mother played with him very gently. But most of the time, she slept.

If Eli became too rough, she slapped him away. Eli would whine and snuggle close to her.

Outside the den, the snow began to melt. Small animals came out of their burrows. Tiny green buds formed on the trees. Frogs croaked. Beneath the snow, tender grass roots sprouted. Each day was a little warmer.

It was time for the she-bear to wake up. She stretched and grunted. She stuck her nose through the opening of the den. It looked safe enough.

She pushed her cub with her nose. He whined as he wobbled ahead. It was time for Eli to learn to be a bear.

Chapter 3

Eli blinked in the bright daylight. He looked all around. He took a step. His feet hurt. He cried out.

Eli didn't like the great outdoors. The light hurt his eyes. And the ground hurt his feet.

The she-bear also whimpered a little. Her feet were very tender. Some bears shed their footpads during the winter denning.

Bears have feet with five toes and very long, sharp claws. They walk with their whole foot flat on the ground. Most animals walk and run on their toes. Bears can walk easily on their hind legs too. Native Americans called bears "Beast that walks like man."

Bears have poor eyesight. They stand on their hind feet to see things better. But they have a strong sense of smell and hearing.

Eli's mother nudged him a little. But he would not go. He turned back toward the opening of the den. He wanted back in his safe, warm place.

The she-bear pushed him with one paw. He bawled.

But finally, on his tender feet, he hobbled along behind his mother.

Soon they stopped. The she-bear's feet throbbed. She sat on her haunches. She took her cub in her arms and nursed him.

Eli suckled noisily. He made humming sounds as he nursed. Drops of milk ran down his chin. When he finished, his mother washed him with her rough tongue.

Eli's fur was darker than his mother's. Black bears can be many colors. Most are black. But they can be tan or brown. Some are cinnamon or rusty brown.

There is one kind of black bear that is nearly white with white claws. It lives in the coastal area of British Columbia.

A very rare bear is the blue bear. Also

called "glacier bear." It has gray hairs mixed with the black ones. This makes a bluish color. The blue bear is only found in a small area in southeastern Alaska. The natives of the area believe that blue bears are sacred.

Eli's mother got to her feet. She started walking slowly. Eli waddled along behind.

Many new smells tickled his nose. He heard many strange sounds. Blue jays squawking. Frogs croaking. Woodpeckers pecking. And wind whistling through the trees.

The she-bear was not hungry. But she was very thirsty. When they came to a small stream, she drank loudly.

Eli's eyes grew wide as he watched. He was too young to drink water. All he needed for now was his mother's milk.

When the mother bear finished drinking, she went on. Eli followed. Several times she woofed at her cub. Telling him to hurry. But he was so tired.

Eli was two months old and weighed a little over eight pounds. He had gained a pound a week.

His short legs ached. He bawled as he tried to keep up.

The she-bear stopped. She had found what she was looking for. Skunk cabbage. Skunk cabbage is a plant that grows in wet places. It has large yellow blooms. It's one of a bear's favorite foods. Especially in the spring.

The she-bear nibbled a few bites of the plant. Eli watched his mother as she chewed. He sniffed at her mouth. It was not a good smell. Food did not interest Eli yet. He only cared for milk.

After a few bites, the she-bear stopped eating. She was not hungry yet. And her stomach could not hold much. Not right away.

She lay down and rolled on her side. Eli quickly crawled between her front legs and began to nurse. He fell asleep. The she-bear dozed a little. But she listened closely to the forest sounds.

There is little danger to a bear except man. And sometimes other bears. An adult male bear will often attack cubs. Even kill them. A mother bear will fight any male bear to protect her cubs. No matter how large.

At the end of the day, the she-bear found a warm spot in a thicket. She curled herself around Eli. They both slept soundly.

Chapter 4

Eli's first day out of the den had been very tiring. And even a little scary. In a few days, the bears' feet had lost their tenderness. Eli was enjoying the forest more and more.

Every day he learned something new.
He learned to drink water. He didn't like
it very much. It didn't taste sweet like
milk. And it was so cold.

He learned to nibble grass and plants.
He shuddered at his first taste of skunk
cabbage.

Eli learned to turn over rocks and lick
up the insects under them. He wasn't
very good at turning over rocks. Once,
a rock came back down on his paw. He
howled loudly. He was more angry than
hurt.

The ants tickled his tongue. He had to
swallow hard to make them go down
his throat.

Eli learned to pull himself over fallen logs. If he got hung up on a log, he bawled. He kicked his feet wildly in midair. But his mother always came to his rescue.

Then one day, Eli learned the best thing of all. He learned to climb trees. The she-bear had a hard time making her cub understand what he was supposed to do.

She pushed and pushed him toward the small pine tree. She stood up and pawed the tree.

At last, he understood. He was supposed to go up that tree. But why?

When he got to the first limb, he stopped. He looked down. His heart raced. And he trembled a little.

The she-bear snuffled at the tree. She stood on her hind legs. She stretched herself as tall as she could. She was nearly as tall as the limb where the cub sat.

Eli stopped trembling. His mama was nearby.

Slowly, he climbed down the tree. Then he climbed up another tree. It was a bigger one. This was the most fun he'd had yet.

One day, he discovered what happened when he disobeyed his mother.

The bears were walking along a forest trail. It was a warm, lazy day.

Suddenly something appeared on the trail ahead of them. It was a small animal covered with stickers. A porcupine!

Eli started toward it. The she-bear

woofed. She was saying, "Come back."

Eli paid no attention. He kept going toward the porcupine.

Again his mother called him. He ignored her.

All at once, Eli's mother smacked him hard with her paw. He rolled on the ground. He got up, bawling. He looked at his mother. She was very angry.

He crept slowly toward her. She picked him up. She held him against her, and he nursed. He made sobbing noises as he swallowed the milk.

Many times, Eli was cuffed for disobeying. Bears who have several cubs spank them often for playing too rough or loud. Or for wandering off. Cubs sound like small children when they bawl.

Eli and his mother napped under an aspen tree. They had just feasted on a meal of roots and beetles.

A rustling sound in the thick underbrush woke the mother and her cub. Out of the brush came a big black male bear. Eli had never seen any bear except his mother. And this bear was huge.

The male bear reared on its hind legs. The she-bear sprang to her feet. She gave a fierce growl. The male bear came toward them.

Eli bawled frantically. His mother woofed a command. Eli knew what it meant. "Climb a tree! Quick!"

In seconds, Eli was at the very top of the tree. He held on for dear life. His heart pounded in his chest. From his perch, he watched. He had never seen his mother so angry. She roared. She clicked her teeth.

The male bear lunged toward her. Eli could see his big teeth. The she-bear swung at the male with an open paw. Her growls grew louder and fiercer.

Suddenly the male bear dropped to all four feet. He turned and ran off through the trees. He grumbled as he ran. The she-bear continued clicking her teeth.

After a while, she grunted for Eli to come down now. The she-bear sniffled his fur. She rubbed her nose against his face. Eli had never felt so safe.

Chapter 5

Eli's first summer was good. There was plenty of food. The kind of food bears like.

Bears are classed as *carnivores*. This means they are meat eaters. But bears eat more berries and nuts than meat.

They like all kinds of roots and fruits from trees. They eat flowers, grass, and some leaves. When berries are ripe, bears eat their fill.

And bears love honey. They will brave a swarm of bees to get it. Bee stings don't bother bears. Their fur is too thick. Bees can only sting a bear's nose. Besides, bears eat the bees too.

Bears eat *carrion*—dead animals. In the fall, they feast on nuts. Especially acorns. They eat bird eggs, snakes, turtles, mice, fish, and frogs.

They love ants. A bear will swat at an anthill with its paw. Then the bear lets the ants crawl up its leg. With its long, rough tongue, the bear licks off the ants.

John Muir was a man who studied wild animals. He once said that to a bear "almost everything is food—except granite."

When Eli and his mother weren't eating, they were sleeping. The more they ate, the sleepier they got.

Once bears leave the den, they never return to it. Bears sleep anywhere. Sometimes they sleep all day. And hunt food at night. It depends on their mood.

Eli loved wandering about at night. He

liked the night sounds. Owls hooting.
Frogs croaking. Crickets chirping.

He liked being with his mother. He
liked listening to her snuffle as she
plodded along.

She hardly ever went too fast for him.
If she did, she scolded him for not
keeping up. Eli would waddle along as
fast as he could.

One sunny morning, Eli amused himself by turning somersaults in the tall grass. He woofed happily as he played all alone.

The she-bear was nearby. She was scratching her back on a pine tree. She grunted loudly as she moved back and forth.

She was shedding her winter hair. It made her itch. She had patches of bare skin. Mosquitoes could bite her on the bare spots.

When she finished scratching, she called to her cub. Eli followed her.

They came to a swamp. The she-bear rolled in the mud. The mud covered her bare spots. It coated her fur. This kept the insects from biting her.

Eli's fur was thick. The insects did not bother him.

Eli ran along the edge of the swamp.

He chased frogs. He woofed at a flicker pecking on a tree. The flicker scolded him.

Suddenly, Eli caught a strange smell. The smell was new to him. Something burned his nose. It made his eyes water.

The she-bear smelled it too. It made her nervous. She stood on her hind legs and looked all around. She made a rumbling sound deep in her throat. She did not like the smell.

It was a smell of smoke. There is nothing more frightening to an animal than fire. Every year, many wild animals are killed in forest fires. Millions of trees are destroyed.

In 1950, a bear cub was badly burned during a forest fire in a national forest in New Mexico. He was found clinging to a burned tree snag. The cub was rescued by the firefighters.

A game warden took the little bear to a doctor. His burns were treated. Then the game warden took him home. He and his wife nursed the cub back to health.

People heard about the bear. He reminded them of Smokey Bear. Until now, Smokey had not been a real bear. He had only been a bear on posters and in ads. He told people to be careful with fires. Especially forest fires.

The bear cub was later sent to the National Zoo in Washington, D.C. People came from all over to see the little bear named Smokey. He was the living Smokey Bear.

The real Smokey lived at the National Zoo until 1976. He died of old age.

The smoke the bears smelled was not from a forest fire. Some distance away, a part of the forest had been logged. The tree limbs had been stacked in piles. They had been set on fire. Wind blew the smoke toward the bears.

But Eli's mother didn't know this. The she-bear grew more and more worried. She called her cub to her. It was time to find a new place to live.

For several days, the bears traveled. Eli grew very tired. They climbed high hills. They crossed a river. Eli swam beside his mother. Bears love water. And they are strong swimmers.

On the other side of the river, they came to an open meadow. It was surrounded by woods. This would be a good place to live. There were trees to climb.

There were thickets of berries. There were rotten logs lying about. They would be full of good grub worms. Nothing was better than fat grub worms.

There were swamps. And a big river. This would be their new home.

Chapter 6

Eli was growing rapidly. By late summer, he weighed over 40 pounds. Every day, the bears stuffed themselves with ripe, juicy berries. They caught mice and frogs. They rolled in the muddy swamps. It was a good life.

Then came the big salmon run. The river was full of fish. Bears came from all over. Big male bears. Mother bears with cubs.

Eli couldn't believe his eyes. He had no idea there were so many other bears in the world. In no time, he was romping and wrestling with cubs his size.

What fun it was! And what a racket! Bear cubs squealed and bawled. Adult bears growled and argued. Fish jumped and splashed in the water.

Salmon season is one of the few times bears gather together. Bears are solitary animals. Except for the time

they spend with their young, bears like to be alone. Especially male bears.

Eli tried catching fish. He wasn't very good at it. He watched his mother and the other bears. They slapped the big fish into the air. They caught them in their sharp teeth.

Eli liked the taste of the fish. He stuffed himself. Then he lay down on the sandy beach and fell asleep.

For days, the bears ate all the fish they could hold.

The wild berries were gone now. It was time for nuts. Eli followed his mother to an oak grove. They ate acorns. Eli loved them. He no longer drank his mother's milk.

It was the end of October. Eli weighed 50 pounds. The days had grown very short. The nights were getting colder. It was nearly time for the bears' winter sleep.

This winter, Eli and his mother would den

together. But the following winter, Eli would be on his own.

His mother would mate the next summer. In the spring, she would give birth to more cubs. She would probably have twins.

Eli would find a new place to live. He would probably never see his mother again.

When he was three or four years old, he would mate. But he would never know his cubs.

Day after day, Eli and his mother filled their stomachs with food. Then they began to search for a den. Bears never use the same den more than once.

At last, they found a good winter den. It was an opening in a rock wall. The opening was partly covered with brush.

The she-bear squeezed inside. She sniffed the ground. There were no

animal smells. She turned around and
around. It was just the right size for a
winter home. Just big enough for the
she-bear and her growing cub.

When Eli left the den in the spring, he

would weigh about 80 to 90 pounds.

He would not reach his full growth until he was about five years old. Bears in the wild can live up to 20 to 25 years.

Every day the bears grew sleepier. Snow fell day and night for a long time. It got colder and colder.

Eli helped his mother carry dry grass and leaves into the den. They carried in some sticks and moss.

Then one dark, cloudy day, they crawled inside. They snuggled together. It was time for their long winter nap.

Eli had learned a lot in less than a year. He had learned to hunt for food. He had learned to climb trees. He had learned to swim and catch fish. He had learned to stay out of danger. Eli had learned how to be a bear.